I'm not your
Friend

For Maralyn – S.McB.

For My Mother – K.L.

First published in hardback in Great Britain by HarperCollins Publishers Ltd in 2001
First published in paperback by Collins Picture Books in 2002

3 5 7 9 10 8 6 4 2

ISBN: 0 00 664690 5

Collins Picture Books is an imprint of the Children's Division, part of HarperCollins Publishers Ltd.

Text copyright © Sam McBratney 2001
Illustrations copyright © Kim Lewis 2001

The HarperCollins website address is: www.fireandwater.com

Manufactured in China.

I'm not your Friend

Sam McBratney

illustrated by Kim Lewis

Collins

An imprint of HarperCollinsPublishers

Once upon a time
there was a little fox.

The little fox and his mother were playing
in the fields. They played running games,
sneak-up-and-pounce games,

and stand-completely-still games; and when their shadows grew long in the evening they played jump-over-my-shadow games.

Then mother fox looked away to where
the sun was going down.

"It's getting late," she said. "We'll stop
playing now and get ready for the night."

The little fox scampered away
through the long grass.
"I'm not coming!" he shouted.
"You have to try and find me."
Mother fox looked over her shoulder.
"It will soon be dark," she said.
"We can play again tomorrow."

But the little fox didn't want to wait until tomorrow. He wanted to play another game and he wanted to play it now.

"I'm not your friend any more," he said.

"And I'm not going to be your friend again…ever."

"Oh dear, you'll never be my friend again?"

"No. Never ever."

The little fox lay very still in the long
grass. Everything was quiet. He watched
some tall meadow plants swaying in the breeze.
 Something fluttered above his head and, looking
up, he saw the early evening stars.
 Could something be watching him?

"Well I won't be your friend for
a long time," he said. "A long long time."
"And how long is a long time?" called his mother.

"Until I'm big."

"Then I shall just have to wait until you're big," sighed his mother.

The little fox glanced over his shoulder. Did he hear whispering behind him, or only the swish of the wind blowing through the meadow grass?

Something could be getting ready to chase me, he thought, something really really nasty with pointy teeth and sharp claws, and his mother wouldn't even know.

"Well... I think I might be your friend tomorrow," he said quietly.

No answer came.
Was his mother still there?
Or was he all alone?

The little fox stood up on his back legs and saw that it *was* getting dark – there were shadows and strange shapes everywhere.

He began to run. He ran and ran from all
the things that might be just behind him!
Then...

Then he saw his mother, waiting
for him in the last of the daylight.

With a rush and a hop the little fox jumped
up and held tight to his mother's soft fur, and
he knew that nothing could get to him now!

"I hope you will be my friend tomorrow," said his mother.

The little fox stretched up to whisper into his mother's ears. There was one more thing that he wanted to say.

"You don't have to wait until tomorrow, I am your friend now."

"Oh good." His mother smiled as the little fox
settled down to sleep.
 "That's very good," she said softly in the dark,
"For I'm your friend, too – and do you
know what? I'll always be
your friend."